INCREDIBLE PONY TALES

CHRISTINE PULLEIN-THOMPSON

CAVALIER PAPERBACKS

Published by Cavalier Paperbacks 1998
Burnham House
Jarvis St
Upavon
Wilts SN9 6DU

ISBN 1-899470-16-6

Printed and bound in Great Britain by Cox &
Wyman, Reading, Berks

CONTENTS

THE ZIG ZAG PONY

My first very own pony arrived in a horsebox. He was thirteen hands high and piebald. Grandad had sent him because he knew I had wanted a pony ever since I was two years old. I was pony mad, Mum said. Incurably mad. As my very own piebald pony backed down the ramp, I cried, "Oh he's so lovely and he's really, really pretty." Grandad wasn't there to be thanked but I would pour out my thanks to him later on the telephone.

"Can I ride him now?" I asked, as my pony looked around.

But Mrs Card, whom we called Pat, and with whom he was to live, said, "Not till tomorrow Susie. He needs at least a day to settle down."

And then I looked at my piebald pony again and said, "I'm going to call him See Saw because his markings remind me of a see-saw. Susie and See Saw are first in the under thirteen two jumping. It sounds really good, doesn't it?"

"Hasn't he got a name already?" asked Pat.

"No. My father bought him nameless at an auction," replied Mum.

"He looks a smashing pony and so sensible and quiet," said Pat leading him towards a loose box. "Ponies like him don't usually turn up at auctions. They are as rare as gold dust."

And I remember thinking that's a really good name for a Palomino – Gold Dust!

"Your Grandad must be a very sensible man," said Pat, "Because looking at this pony, I don't think I could have chosen you anything better, Susie."

"Well for years he was a farrier," replied Mum. "In fact he's only just retired and like Susie here he's always been mad about horses."

"But why a good pony like this should go to auction beats me. They are usually snapped up in a trice," said Pat.

If we had listened to Pat we should have heard alarm bells ringing then, but we didn't. All Mum said was, "Well my old Dad has always had an eye for a horse."

I was nine with fairish hair cut in a fringe. Dad was away working, but we told him all about See Saw that evening when he telephoned. I spoke to Grandad on the phone as well, thanking him over and over again for See Saw.

The next day I rode See Saw in Pat's paddock. I had ridden since I was six, once a week at a riding school, so I wasn't a beginner.

I knew straightaway that See Saw was better than any pony I had ever ridden before – full of life, but easy to control. He didn't need to be kicked along, just a squeeze with one's calves was enough to make him go faster. Pat lent me some tack – an egg butt snaffle and a saddle with a leather girth and safety stirrups. It was a Friday and the middle of the Easter holidays, the sun was shining, the birds were singing and I was so happy that I felt like crying.

Next day Mum suggested we ride out. "I will come with you on my bike. I need the exercise," she said.

Pat was away for the day. See Saw opened his mouth for his bit and stood patiently while I saddled him. The sun was shining again and See Saw seemed really pleased to be going somewhere. He had a marvellous long striding walk and his funny piebald ears were pricked in front of me as we set off, and I kept thinking, he's mine, he's really mine. Oh I'm so lucky.

"Heels down. Sit up," Mum called imitating Jo Street my instructor at the riding school.

"They are and I am," I laughed.

A second later See Saw stopped and then after smelling the air, broke into a trot.

"Hey, not too fast, I don't want to get left behind," called Mum pedalling furiously.

I pulled on See Saw's reins, but nothing happened. I pulled again and he simply went faster."

"Wait for me, Susie," shouted Mum. "Slow down will you – please."

"I'm trying to, but he won't slow down," I shouted back.

"Then turn him round," yelled Mum, "Go on pull."

Her voice sounded frightened now so that I knew she was thinking of the main road less than half a mile away. I pulled and pulled, but See Saw simply put down his head and went faster and faster until the trot became a canter and then a gallop. I felt all shaky now and my legs felt weak and useless and the harder I pulled on the reins the harder See Saw pulled back. It had become a tug of war and I was losing it. The main road was quite near now, and I couldn't hear Mum's voice any more. Everything was quiet except for the sound of See Saw's hoofs on the narrow tarmac road. On each side of me stretched fields empty except for the crops growing there. I started to shout, "Whoa, See Saw. Stop. Whoa."

Then I could see the main road, but just before we reached it See Saw gave a loud neigh and turned left along a drive-way I had never noticed before.

I was holding only the end of his reins now and my legs had gone back and were clutching See Saw's sides so that without meaning to, I was urging him to go faster.

There was no sound from Mum; all I could hear was the sound of a dog barking. Then See Saw slowed to a trot and I saw a stable yard ahead of me with ponies looking over loose box doors and upturned buckets; then See Saw stopped so abruptly that I went straight on over his head onto the concrete yard.

At the same moment a girl's voice started to shout, "Mum, Mum, Zig Zag's here. He's come home. He's back here. It's a miracle.

I wasn't hurt badly. I stood up and said, "He's not Zig Zag, he's called See Saw and he belongs to me."

"No, he doesn't. He's mine but are you all right?" asked the girl who was taller than I was and probably older.

"Yes. But See Saw's mine. Grandad gave him to me," I shouted. "He bought him for me. Okay?"

"He's a thief then," replied the girl, taking hold of See Saw's reins. "A horrible, horrible thief."

Holding onto See Saw's reins, I shouted again, "He's mine and he's called See Saw, not Zig Zag. I'm Susie and he's See Saw."

"And I'm Zoe, and he's Zig Zag," retorted the girl holding onto See Saw's bridle.

Our mothers arrived then, Zoe's from the house and Mum puffing, red in the face and exhausted on her old bike.

They looked at each other before Mum said, "I thought they were going to get on the main road and be killed. It was terrifying. I don't know what got into the pony. He was so perfect yesterday."

"He is perfect," said Zoe.

"He's come here because this is his home," replied her mother who turned out to be called Maureen. "He was stolen six weeks ago. We should have had him freeze-marked with a number, but we didn't."

"It was my fault. I didn't want to spoil his zig zags," confessed Zoe.

"Put him in the stable Zoe and then everyone come inside and have a coffee. We need to talk," said Maureen.

Zoe's brother, Richard was making coffee for himself in the untidy kitchen. He was tall and really cool. "So Zig Zag's come home," he said. "What a clever pony."

"It's a miracle," said Zoe again, throwing herself down onto a sofa. Then Richard showed us a photo of Zig Zag with Zoe riding him holding the largest rosette you've ever seen and an enormous cup.

"It was taken last summer. We won the jumping and the Best Pony Class that day," said Zoe.

Mum and Maureen drank coffee and talked. Maureen said that because Zig Zag had been stolen he still belonged to them. "I'm sorry, but that's the law," she said.

I was trying not to cry. I had fallen on my shoulder and it hurt. And suddenly See Saw wasn't mine anymore. Zoe gave me a drink; but I didn't want it. I wanted to disappear, to disappear and wake up and know that what was happening now was no more than a bad dream and that See Saw was still mine.

Mum was talking, telling them about Grandad living two hundred miles away and how he wouldn't have known that See Saw, or now Zig Zag, had been stolen. "He bought him in good faith," she said.

"But he's still ours because he was stolen," replied Maureen. "Besides Susie can't manage him can she? Because if she could you wouldn't be here now."

And Mum had no answer to that.

"I want to ring my husband. He's in France but I have his number," she said after a moment. "I will pay for the call, of course."

Dad is a solicitor and knows all about stolen goods and the law. Mum talked to him for ages. When she returned to the sitting room, her face wasn't red any more, it was ashen.

"We had better go. But first we want the pony's tack," she announced in a dignified voice. "You see it isn't ours. It belongs to Pat Card."

The atmosphere changed when she

mentioned Pat Card. "Oh well, if you are keeping your pony with Pat Card, that's different," said Maureen.

"What about Tramp. He needs a good home," suggested Richard, smiling.

"Yes, he would be fine," agreed Zoe.

"Shall we give Alice a ring?" asked Richard.

"Why not. I'll do it," shouted Zoe, running to the telephone in the hall.

"What's going on now," asked Mum and I saw for the first time that she was crying and that started me off again.

"They are finding you a pony. He's called Tramp. He's not as pretty as Zig Zag, but he's very, very reliable," said Maureen. "And he's looking for a good home and if you will be keeping him with Pat Card, well, that is a good home."

But Tramp's owners were out.

Maureen offered to drive us home, but we refused the offer. We went together taking it in turns to ride the bike.

"Grandad's going to be very upset," said Mum.

"What will Pat say when she hears?" I wondered.

The road home seemed shorter than it had been galloping on Zig Zag.

"He won't get me another pony now will he? I mean he's lost all the money he spent," I said.

"He may be able to sue someone. He may even get them sent to prison, which will be an excellent thing," said Mum.

"Dad will be home tomorrow and he'll sort it out."

I spent a terrible night. My shoulder ached and I kept dreaming that everything had been a mistake and that See Saw was back in Pat's field and really mine after all. And of course when I woke up I knew my dream wasn't true.

Dad came home and said that we hadn't a leg to stand on and that Grandad had been a fool, which annoyed me and Mum no end. I was miserable and cross now and terribly disappointed.

But then two days later Pat banged on our backdoor. "I've got a pony on loan for you, Susie. He's called Tramp. Come and look," she said.

Tramp was dark bay with a star on his forehead and three white fetlocks. He whinnied when he saw me. He had lovely dark eyes and a very thick shiny tail.

"You are very lucky having him on loan," said Pat. "I know Tramp well and he's a great pony, and he won't gallop along the road with you either, Susie."

"So you know what happened?" I asked.

"Of course, news travels and Zoe and Richard have been marvellous and absolutely determined to find you a pony," said Pat.

And so Tramp has become my pony for a time at least. He is quieter than Zig Zag; and I know whatever happens he will never take off with me.

Tramp isn't a very nice name, but I suppose I'm stuck with it.

I call him Trampie and sometimes Zoe and I ride out together and Zoe says she's really pleased that Grandad bought me Zig Zag because otherwise she might never have seen him again.

As for Grandad, the wheels of the law turn slowly, or so Mum says. But he may get the money he paid for Zig Zag back one day and then he says he'll put it away somewhere safe for my next

pony; but this time he won't go to an
auction to find it.

A HORSEY WITCH

CHAPTER ONE

"I'm not going to win the twelve and under jumping at the show on Saturday because Jessica Hawtrey has been lent a brilliant pony which can jump one and a half metres. Are you listening Milly?" asked Peter who was lolling in a chair in the living room. Milly was pushing an electric cleaner across the patterned carpet there. She was a home help and she doted on Peter. People said that she loved him as though he was her own son, the son she had never had. Milly had a long nose and a bent back and whiskers on her chin. She lived by herself and she knew everything which was going on in the village of Branhill.

"Poor pet. What a shame. What can we do about it?" she asked switching off the cleaner.

"Make Jessica's new pony lame. Let it out. Cripple it," replied Peter who was really rather a nasty boy. "But how? That's the point, Milly. I don't want to be caught and go to prison or some other disgusting place where there's only porridge for breakfast."

"Certainly not," replied Milly thoughtfully. "But I'm getting a brilliant idea in my old head, just wait a minute will you? It isn't ripe yet, but it's ripening."

Peter lay back in his chair and imagined himself winning on his pony, Pimpernel, who was the colour of a polished conker with black points. In his mind he saw his parents and their friends watching him accept a silver cup from a local dignitary and in his head he heard a quiet respectful clapping. At last he would be living up to his father's expectations, for in his younger days his father had been a racing driver and he believed in entering competitions to win; he didn't believe in losers. And Peter was certain he could win until he had heard about Jessica being lent the well known jumper Barney, a pony which had never stopped at a fence in his entire life.

"It's all right I know what we will do," said Milly. "I'll go and see Lena Appleby for you. She can fix anything. But she will need paying."

"How much?" Peter was sitting up now. Everyone had heard of Lena Appleby. Some called her a witch. She lived alone at the end of a long lane in a tumbledown cottage where visitors were not welcome.

"Quite a lot. I'm afraid she won't do anything for nothing. It's risky you see and she has her expenses," replied Milly.

Peter remembered the gold sovereign his Grandfather had left him in his will, which was upstairs in his bedroom in a box lined with velvet. Next he imagined Jessica winning first prize on Barney, smiling as she received the silver cup, cameras whirring, her picture in the local paper. He imagined his father's disappointed face and the feeling that he had failed him again, just as he did at Maths, at football, at pretty well everything.

"She can have my sovereign, Milly. I don't need it," he said. "But she can't have it until she's done whatever she has to do. Okay, Milly?"

"Fair enough. It will be done," replied Milly switching on the cleaner.

Jessica could hardly take her eyes off Barney. She loved her old pony, Toffee, but Barney was in a different league. Barney was part-thoroughbred with a head to fit, a large knowing eye, and long slender legs. Jessica who wore her fair hair tied back behind her ears really didn't mind about winning prizes – though she had won fifty or more on Toffee but only for Gymkhana events and Family Pony classes. She had never ridden Toffee at the show on Saturday which was grander than any show she had ever entered before. Jessica's greatest fear was that she would let Barney down, because when his owner had handed him over he had said, "I expect you to win the cup on Saturday, Jessica. Just give Barney his head and he'll do the rest."

And Jessica knew that what he said was true. If she rode properly, she might even beat stuck up Peter Longman on his two thousand pound pony Pimpernel, and she wanted to beat Peter because no one liked him, because he never spoke to anyone, but rode around looking better than anyone else.

But on Wednesday morning when Jessica went to give Barney his breakfast she had a terrible shock. He was standing miserably in his loose box holding up his off foreleg and he looked in terrible pain. He wouldn't even look at his breakfast which was full of lovely things liked chopped golden delicious apples and new spring carrots. Crying, Jessica fetched her mother. "How can it have happened?" wailed her mother. "I'll ring for a vet but it will be no jumping for you on Saturday."

"I don't care about Saturday. I only care about poor Barney. What can have happened? He was fine yesterday. What will his owner say? I feel dreadful. I feel sick," said Jessica.

"These things happen," replied her mother biting her nails with anxiety.

The vet came. He was tall with a rugged face and large capable hands.

Barney was nervous. He backed away and putting his ears back, bared his teeth.

"What's the matter with you then?" asked the vet who was called Mr Moore.

Jessica put on Barney's head-collar and held him, while Mr Moore picked up Barney's slim chestnut off foreleg.

"Well, he's got a nail driven into his hoof for starters. And it looks deliberate. Have you got any enemies?" he asked.

"Only a few girls at school," replied Jessica.

"It wouldn't be a few girls who did this. It was someone who has a way with horses or is very strong. I'm appalled," said Mr Moore easing the nail out with a large pair of tweezers. "Poor old fellow. No wonder you are nervous."

"He's had his anti-tetanus jab," said Mum.

"Good. Well done," replied Mr Moore. "I'm going to give him a long lasting antibiotic; then we'll put a dressing on. But I should keep him under lock and key until you find the culprit of this dastardly deed."

"So he won't be better by the show on Saturday?" asked Jessica without much hope in her voice.

"You must be joking," replied Mr Moore. "He's going to be off work for several weeks and then he'll need to be shod with a leather under his shoe."

Jessica cried all evening. She cried because Barney was miserable and because his owner, whom Mum had telephoned, was angry, and because whatever anyone said she felt that it was all her fault – which it wasn't. Her mother rang the police and explained what had happened to Barney, but they said that they were stretched to the limit investigating three arson attacks, and that it was only an isolated incident. And to keep all gates and stables locked in future and that they would send out a warning to the horse owners in the area. That was all. Jessica felt terribly let down. "I think two people died in one of the arson attacks, so it is more important. And what happened to poor Barney does seem far fetched," Mum said.

Peter handed Milly his precious gold

sovereign.

"Please thank Mrs Appleby. Everyone seems to know that Jessica's pony is lame, so I don't need to check. It's brilliant," he said.

"She's not a Mrs, she's a Ms," replied Milly with a cackle. "I'm glad to be of service to you. And you can count on me being there to watch you on Saturday, pet. I'll be there cheering you on. And your Dad will be over the moon with joy. He won't be able to call you a loser any more, not when you have that silver cup on the mantelpiece with your name engraved on it. He'll be so proud of you, Peter."

But by a strange coincidence Pimpernel was lame on Thursday. Peter was beside himself with worry and rage. Milly comforted him. "Lena Appleby will put it right. Don't you worry pet. She'll see him tonight and in the morning he'll be sound, take my word for it," she said.

"But how?" demanded Peter.

"That's her secret," replied Milly.

"She's a witch isn't she?" asked Peter.

"Some say that," replied Milly. "I like to think she's a horsey witch and that's a rare witch."

Peter didn't dare tell his parents that Pimpernel was lame. Peter didn't even dare call a vet.

Milly was putting on her coat to leave when Peter said, "But I haven't any money to give Ms Appleby. It's all gone until Saturday and then it's only a pound if Dad actually remembers my pocket money."

Buttoning up her coat Milly said, "You can give her the silver cup you'll be winning. She'll like that. We'll wait a few days and then it will disappear and you can say it has been stolen. Don't you worry your little head, pet, Milly will see to everything.

"But that's lying," replied Peter.

"And that won't be the first time, will it, Peter?" added Milly with another dreadful cackle.

"But what will she do to Pimpernel?" asked Peter next.

"She'll use one of her potions to make him better. And don't you start crying about it, because if you do your Mum will want to know the reason why," said Milly. "Now just you have a good night's rest and when you wake up again everything will be all right."

"Are you sure?"

"Yes, your pony will be fine and everyone will be happy."

And in the morning Pimpernel really was sound again. It's like a miracle thought Peter happily. The only sign of treatment was a few scabs on

Pimpernel's off foreleg and that he seemed rather nervous.

Milly told Peter to rub some black shoe polish into the leg.

"It's lucky his leg is black, because if it were white we would be in trouble," she said laughing.

Peter didn't answer. He was starting to grow tired of Milly and a little afraid too, because if Milly started talking about how she had helped him, he could be in trouble. It didn't take a fool to see that. Peter was beginning to feel sick with worry and an awful sense of guilt. So, as he groomed Pimpernel on the morning of the show, he was feeling knotted up inside. And supposing I don't win? he thought. Everything will have been in vain then. I won't have a silver cup to give the old witch as payment and my gold sovereign will have been wasted.

Peter dressed in his best riding clothes for the show, which was really rather an important one. He put on his new black riding jacket, his cream jodhpurs, and his black boots. He persuaded Milly to tie his tie which had stripes on it and he didn't forget his head gear, which was the latest and safest money could buy.

In the yard his parents were packing their car with a hamper full of goodies.

"Wow, you look smart Peter," exclaimed his mother.

"You go out there and win," said his father slapping him on the back.

Pimpernel seemed unusually on edge when the horsebox arrived. A girl groom called Louise had arrived earlier to plait his mane. "He knows he's going somewhere," she said smiling, "but what's he done to his leg?"

"He scraped it in the stable, I don't know how," lied Peter.

"You are so lucky having him. But why are you so downhearted. You look really sad," asked Louise. "Now that poor Jessica is out of it, you're certain to win."

Peter didn't answer because he didn't know what to say.

As well as plaiting Pimpernel's mane, Louise had bandaged all four of his legs and his tail. His rug had Peter's initials on it – PHL, Peter Henry Longman. His hoofs were newly oiled and his mane and tail looked as fine as silk.

CHAPTER TWO

Before she set off for the show, Jessica locked Barney's loose box doors. "I'm sorry. I know it's awful being shut in, but we can't risk you being hurt again by a madman," she told him sadly as she closed the top one. Barney was wearing a poultice on his injured hoof. But he was standing on it now and in a few days he might be sound again, but Jessica knew that she would only be able to ride him quietly for a long time.

Lena Appleby was also getting ready to go to the Horse Show. She had placed the sovereign in its velvet lined case on the mantelpiece, now she hid it under the cushion on her only armchair. She was looking forward to seeing the cup that would soon be hers and she was considering having her own name engraved on it just for fun. She had fed her many animals – her thirteen black cats, her tame toads, her ten white mice and her nine grey rats. She had pinned up her straggly grey hair, which was never washed, and put on her best scarlet dress, her long black coat and her little pointed black ankle boots. She wore no stockings and her long thin legs looked old and dirty as she mounted her ancient bicycle.

By the time Lena Appleby arrived at the show, the twelve year and under jumping class had begun. Waiting to go in, Peter had butterflies in his stomach, while Jessica leaned against the ring ropes imagining that she was about to compete herself on Barney.

When Lena Appleby appeared beside her Jessica was deciding how she would have taken each fence.

"Is it all right if I stand here?" asked Lena Appleby in her croaky voice.

"Yes, of course," replied Jessica. "You can stand where you like."

Lena Appleby smelt. She smelt of old potato peelings, of cat mess, toad mess, and of unwashed body. Jessica was too polite to hold her nose or move away. She was afraid she might upset Lena and she didn't like upsetting people.

"Do you think young Peter Longman will win?" asked Lena.

"I expect so," replied Jessica.

"It's a pity about your pony being lame, ain't it?"

"Yes, terrible," replied Jessica as the loudspeaker announced: "The next competitor is number 17, Peter Longman riding Pimpernel."

And now Jessica noticed Peter's parents sitting on expensive chairs watching.

As Peter approached the first fence Jessica wondered how the old woman standing next to her knew about Peter and about Barney being lame.

"Young Peter Longman will win the silver cup, you'll see," said Lena nudging Jessica with a bony elbow.

Pimpernel was going beautifully. He jumped each fence smoothly clearing it by at least 10 cm. Gradually Peter grew more confident. He forgot about Jessica and Milly and the woman he now thought of as a witch. He forgot about everything but the fences – the brush, the combination, the gate, the upright poles, and the wall. They came and went so easily that it seemed like a dream. There were just three fences left to jump, as he rode towards the parallel bars.

Meanwhile his parents were laughing with their friends and with no other clear round so far, the silver cup seemed almost won.

Unfortunately Lena Appleby, her face screwed up with excitement, was now leaning against the ring ropes on the far side of the parallel bars.

Pimpernel saw her out of the corner of his left eye and remembering the twitch she had put on his nostrils last night and the cruel stinging potion she had poured on his injured leg and the pain which had followed, he stopped and stared at her, before giving a piercing snort. Then he reared up on his hind legs and swinging round bolted from the ring.

Jessica saw it all, "What did you do?" she screamed at the old woman, but Lena Appleby had already gone, scuttling across the show ground like a tatty old bird.

As for Peter, he broke into uncontrollable sobs. Jessica ran after him, "It really doesn't matter, Peter. Don't get upset. It isn't the end of the world. There will be another show, another day, another cup," she cried. "Poor Pimpernel was frightened by that horrible woman. I don't think she meant to frighten him. She wanted you to win. He must have smelt her and she didn't smell very nice. Oh Peter I'm so sorry."

Peter couldn't speak. He could only think, if I hadn't been so awful to Jessica we might both be receiving rosettes now and it wouldn't have mattered who was first and who was second, or only to Dad.

Throwing himself off Pimpernel he cried, "You don't understand Jessica, it's all my fault. I wanted to win so much. I was actually pleased when Barney went lame and now I'm being paid back."

And now half of him wanted to tell Jessica the whole story, but the other half was too afraid of what Lena Appleby might do to Pimpernel if he did, and that if Jessica knew she would never speak to him again.

Peter's parents tried to comfort him. But he was sure they were really thinking – Typical Peter. A born loser if there ever was one.

As for Milly who really loved Peter, she brought back the gold sovereign the next day and gave it to him. But of course their friendship was over, because whenever Peter looked at Milly he remembered what had happened and was filled with remorse.

After that dreadful day Peter and Jessica became friends. And gradually Peter changed. He began to laugh at himself and to say, "I'm a born loser and absolutely hopeless at everything. I may look cool, but I'm the biggest prat on earth." And the more he said it the less it seemed to matter.

Later that summer Peter and Jessica did compete against each other and tied for first place, each clocking up forty seconds in the jump off.

As for Lena Appleby, though she went on being a part time witch, she never meddled with horses again. And Milly, knowing that Peter didn't like her any more, stopped working for the Longmans.

Sometimes now Peter wonders whether Lena and Milly could have been the same person. He had only caught a fleeting glimpse of Lena at the show, but she had had the same sort of whiskers on her chin and a long pointed nose just like Milly.

At other times he's sure they are identical twins. Peter would like to talk about how awful he was and about Lena Appleby to someone. But he doesn't want people to know how cruel he was. So he's waiting till he's much older and then he plans to tell his grandchildren all about the horsey witch and how badly he behaved – if he has any of course.

A SPOOKY RIDE

The caravan site was high above the sea. Below angry waves threw themselves tirelessly against grey rock and shingle. All around the land was flat and peaty; the roads straight and rough; huge prehistoric boulders lay scattered as though carelessly dropped by giants amidst the wiry grass and heather. Donkeys wandered loose and men in dark suits rode ancient bicycles along empty roads.

Half a mile from the site was a farm where horses and ponies looked out of old railway carriages converted into stables. Spilt straw and hay lay scattered across a cobbled yard. Hens scratched busily, while a dog lay chained in the sun.

Sue and Kelly Pinter had just arrived at the stables each carrying a riding hat. They had only arrived at the caravan site yesterday straight from a new housing estate in a new town.

"We've come to ride. Can we hire two ponies?" asked Sue who had long fair hair, a square forehead and brown eyes. Kelly was smaller, younger, and tougher having spent much of her short life trying to keep up with Sue who was three years older than she was.

The farmer was old with weathered cheeks. "You want to ride, do you? Well, can you? That's the big question," he asked laughing.

"Yes, we've ridden quite a lot," replied Sue.

"We can canter and jump, and we

don't mind falling off," added Kelly.

"And how am I to know you're speaking the truth?" the farmer asked.

"Look we've got hats, and proper riding boots," answered Sue as though this would settle the question.

"So you have, but maybe you bought them yesterday. Never mind. I'll let you have a try. You can have the old grey mare," he said pointing at Sue. "And your sister can have the little bay; he's only two and as weak as a kitten."

The bay swayed as he walked. He was too young to be ridden but the girls didn't know that. The old grey had wide sprawling feet and scarred knees. Their saddles pressed on their withers, and none of the tack had seen saddle soap for a long time.

"You'll be safe as houses on them," smiled the farmer. "Now don't be too long," he said tightening their girths and then slapping the ponies on their rumps, said, "Have a good time now."

Kelly and Sue had never ridden on their own before. "Gosh I feel grown up," said Kelly. "Just like the lady who takes us out at the riding school at home."

"You look quite different. She's got a hook nose. But I know what you mean," answered Sue laughing.

Blossom didn't want to leave the farm and wouldn't trot and the bay that was called Tommy, wandered from side to side like young horses do.

"We need whips," said Sue.

"And spurs," said Kelly.

"What would Mum say if she could see us riding on our own, I wonder," commented Sue. "She might be very angry," Kelly said.

"Or she might be very proud," countered Sue.

"We'll be able to tell everyone at school that we rode on our own."

"They won't believe us," Sue said kicking Blossom with her heels.

The road wound straight between wire fences. On each side the ground was marshy and in one place men were cutting peat.

After a time they came to a cross-roads. "Let's go left here," suggested Kelly.

"Okay." Sue didn't mind where she went.

They kicked their ponies into a trot. Blossom's shoes clinked on the road. Tommy wandered from side to side.

"I wish they would go a bit faster," complained Kelly.

They couldn't see the sea any more. They rode over a bridge and passed two donkeys carrying peat on their backs. A ruined house stood alone on the moor. Black-faced sheep muttered like people in their sleep. "We must have been about fifteen minutes so far," said Sue. "I wish we could canter." But now Blossom was stopping. She put her head up and whinnied. Then she stopped altogether.

"Whatever's the matter now?" asked Kelly. "Kick her, Sue. You know what

Miss Roberts at the riding school says. "Legs. Use your legs."

"I am," answered Sue hitting Blossom with the end of the reins. "But she's seen something. I don't know what. A minute ago she felt half dead, now she seems mesmerised!"

"Listen there's a strange noise," said Kelly. "Listen, it isn't the wind. And it isn't the sea because that's too far away. It's a sucking noise...." And then they heard a thick choking cry ....

"But there's nothing there," cried Sue. "Just the moor. And I hate it now."

Blossom neighed again. Her head was high and she was trembling all over. "There's nothing there," said Sue. "What's the matter, Blossom? Steady, steady. It's all right old girl."

"But there's someone calling," cried Kelly. "Listen! It's from the ruins over there. Oh, I'm scared Sue. Let's go back."

Blossom was sweating now. Sue turned her round and then in a flash they were galloping faster than she had ever been before, back towards the farm.

She could hear Kelly calling, "Stop, please stop." But Blossom had her head between her knees now and was galloping faster than had seemed possible a moment ago, and now she wasn't an old pony any more. She seemed young and frisky whereas Tommy was too weak to keep up. He tried, but then tripped and fell and his thin bay knees dripped blood onto the rough road, while Kelly forced her feet out of the stirrups which were too small and stood up beside him. Her nose was scraped and one elbow was bleeding through her shirt. She pulled Tommy to his feet and straightened the saddle.

Then she tied her handkerchief round the worst of his knees and started to walk towards the farm calling, "Wait Sue. Come back. Tommy's hurt."

We shouldn't have gone out alone. We aren't good enough, she thought. And poor Tommy is too thin and Blossom too tired. They are not fit to be ridden. We should have waited for Mum and Dad to come. They said wait, but Sue will never wait. Oh dear, what will happen now? Kelly wondered.

Sue was pulling with all her might on the stiff, cracked reins she still held in her hands. She shouted, "Whoa," and prayed to God for more strength. And then she thought I've let Kelly down. I was in charge and look at me now. And where's Kelly?

The next moment Blossom was galloping into the farm yard where she stopped with a grating of hoofs on cobbles and a flash of sparks. Sue lost her stirrups and then fell slowly into the muck heap. She looked up to see her parents staring at her in horror.

"Where's Kelly?" they cried. "What have you done with Kelly? Why didn't you wait for us? We said to wait."

They all looked wrong in the yard, too tidy, too townish, people from a world of pavements and gleaming motor cars, of tidy houses with garages attached and green mown lawns. Sue's hat and face were covered with dirty straw now and horse muck.

"I don't know," she said. "Blossom wouldn't go. She reached the bridge and then over the other side she went mad…"

"Where is Kelly," asked her father, his fists clenched.

"You should never have gone that way," said the farmer. "Blossom saw the ghost. It was her mother she saw, truly. Didn't I tell you which way to go...?"

"No."

"It was like this," began the farmer ungirthing Blossom's saddle. "We don't want to know what it was like, we only want our other daughter," shouted Mr Pinter angrily.

"Now don't you go worrying, the pony will bring her home unharmed..." replied the farmer leading Blossom away.

"I shall go mad in a minute," said Mrs Pinter, before they heard slow wandering hoof beats. Another minute and Kelly appeared leading Tommy.

"Poor Tommy fell down, just look at his knees," she said.

"Aye, they're not too bad," said the farmer returning. "Just a little grazed. I'll bathe them in a minute. They saw the ghost. That was it. You should never have gone over the bridge. I thought you knew the way," he said accusingly.

"I'm sorry," said Kelly. "We only came yesterday."

"It was like this," began the farmer.

"Wait," said Sue to her parents, who were trying to leave. "Please wait."

"What for?" asked her father rudely. "The old man's mad. Whoever believes in ghosts. And I'm not paying him, not a soul!"

"We want to hear," repeated Kelly standing fair and square. "We want to know why we fell off and anyway I believe in ghosts, and fairies, and elfs, and goblins and everything, the whole lot."

"And I want to hear too," said Sue. "Because there *was* something at the side of the road."

"It's like this," said the farmer taking

off his cap. "Horses have different sight to us. We don't see everything, not by a long way, their hearing is better too, they hear things we have no inkling of, truly."

"Your face is filthy, Sue," complained her mother.

"Go on," said Kelly. "Please go on."

"Look at your arms and your nose. They're bloody, Kelly," said Mr Pinter.

"I don't care," said Kelly. "Please go on."

"Have you got the time?" asked the farmer. "Because it's a story worth hearing."

"Of course we have," cried Kelly.

"It will soon be told," he continued while the girls' parents paced the yard as though they had a train to catch.

It happened like this. There was an old mare here, much like old Blossom there, her Grandmother in fact. She was a bit bigger and a mare of all trades, you understand, but nervous and inclined to shy, you know the sort. Well, my old Dad wanted some drink fetched from a mile or more away (he was a terrible man for drink) and he sent this lad on the old mare to fetch it.

He was a nice lad just turned thirteen and the apple of his mother's eye. Of course they left school at thirteen in those days you understand. So this lad sets off on the old mare bareback with her in nothing but a rope halter. When she gets over the bridge a bit of paper flies up, and she makes a run for it; There was no fence then and she was so scared she didn't see the bog. You saw the ruins, did you? Well an old lady lived there then but she was confined to a wheelchair you understand and there was no telephone then you know. She called for help of course, but no one heard. She screamed and beat on the ground with her stick and while she sat there the boy and the pony were sucked down into the bog. It was a terrible thing, and now the horses don't like going that way, particularly Blossom. It's my belief that she can see her Grandmother in the bog being sucked down and never coming up again."

"Mine too," said Sue.

"Couldn't anyone get them out?" asked Kelly.

"No one knew. They thought the boy had stolen the mare. Then in the evening the old lady's sister called to see her and raised the alarm. But it was too late and neither the boy nor the mare were ever seen again," the farmer said.

"And, I know it's true," insisted Sue,

because Blossom did see something today. She was sweating and neighing and terrified."

"And there were strange noises," added Kelly.

"So our kids could have gone into a bog and never returned," shouted Mr Pinter angrily.

"No, not nowadays. It's been fenced ever since that dreadful day," replied the farmer.

"But Blossom can still see them," Sue said. "Poor Blossom."

"And we heard a cry and a terrible sucking noise. A horrible noise which I shall never forget not as long as I live," cried Kelly.

"You are coming back to the site with us this very minute," said Mr Pinter. "You will never ride here again."

"Fair enough," replied the farmer. "I gave up the horse business years ago.

I only opened today to oblige your girls."

And now Sue could see how old he was, as old as the hills and the bogs and the sea. He belonged to the strange landscape. They were the aliens.

"Yes, let's get back to the site," Sue agreed shivering. "I don't think I know what's real any more."

THE HAUNTED STABLE

"I want to look inside the stable, just once, please Mum, it'll be knocked down tomorrow and you know how I love history. And I want to tell Matt about it, he's asked and asked what it's like inside," said Jack.

Matt was Jack's best friend. His father bred horses and Matt had his own pony. "If you ask again, I'll scream. All right, just this once. But be careful, and remember the stable doesn't belong to us," replied his mother relenting at last.

Just this once thought Jack. Well, I'm hardly likely to go there tomorrow when it'll just be a heap of rubble; or later when it's a modern house thought Jack, finding a coat, his wellies and a torch.

It was almost dark outside. If only Matt was with me, thought Jack running down the drive to the old building which had once been a stable.

Jack hesitated for a moment before pushing open the heavy stable door.

He switched on his torch. He already had an idea how it would look with stalls and maybe brick floors and brass rings. But inside everything was swathed in cobwebs. Jack stood staring as the door ominously closed behind him.

"So you're back from school, Master Jeremy," said a voice. "It's good to see you suddenly grown so tall; but there have been changes, sad changes – since you were last here. Kingfisher and Duke and Highwayman have all been taken to fight in the war. And Will, my right hand man, has gone too."

"Who are you?" demanded Jack in a scared voice.

"Ned. You haven't forgotten me Master Jeremy, have you? Ned, your Uncle's head groom."

"I'm not Jeremy and I'm not master anything, I'm plain Jack Palmer," replied Jack.

A small boy emerged from the shadows. He was shabbily dressed with boots too large for him held together by string.

"And here's Tom, my new helper. Since Will was took away, there's just the two of us here. And only the four horses you see – Meg and Maggy and Blossom and Warrior. They were considered too old to go to war."

Jack looked at the four horses tied up in stalls.

"Don't you ever let them go? And why have their tails been cut off?" he asked.

"Bless you Master Jeremy, they're cut off because that's the way they're wanted. Docked that's what we call them. Nobody wants long tails. They would only get tangled with the harness, stands to reason, don't it?" replied Ned.

"Their hay racks are too high," complained Jack. "Can't you see bits of hay are falling into their eyes? And why don't you do something about the cobwebs – my mother would have a fit if she saw them."

"Well that's a lie. You know as well as I do, that your mother's been dead these twelve months and as for the cobwebs Master Jeremy, we need them to staunch wounds, a handful will stop the bleeding quicker than any bandage and help the healing. And when a horse starts coughing, we put a handful in his feed, and that clears it quicker than you can say Jack Robinson," said Ned.

"But it's so unhygienic," complained Jack. "Why don't you get a vet out and some proper medicine?"

"A vet? What's a vet? We have the
farrier, but your Uncle wouldn't want
to pay him, not when a few cobwebs
would do the trick, Master Jeremy."

"I think you're mixing me up with
someone else. I am NOT and never
have been Master Jeremy," said Jack
irritably.

"Come into the harness room, you
must be famished after your long
journey. But don't walk behind the
'osses. Never walk behind a 'oss unless
you want to be kicked," said Ned.

Following Ned and Tom through a
side door into a room hung with
harness, Jack recalled the horses at
Matt's place, standing in airy loose
boxes, galloping loose in railed
paddocks, eating out of hay-nets.
Suddenly he hated the old stable, with
its imprisoned horses standing hour

after hour in their stalls.

"Of course horses kick if they are tied up all day," he said disagreeably. "Don't you ever turn them loose anywhere?"

"Can't do it in the winter because they get too dirty. And the fields are ploughed up now for the war effort, Master Jeremy but you can speak to your Uncle about it if you like."

"My Uncle lives in America," replied Jack, "and he's not interested in horses."

But Ned wasn't listening because the next thing he said was, "Was your train on time and did you get one of those modern taxicabs from the station Master Jeremy," and he dusted a chair for Jack to sit on.

Tom had lit a lantern, and hung it from a hook in the ceiling. Looking at Jack's torch he asked, "What's that then Master Jeremy?"

"A torch. Haven't you ever seen one before," asked Jack and was about to hand it to him, when his small grubby hand suddenly wasn't there any more or only its outline, so that for the first time Jack thought, they're ghosts. All ghosts.

"And I like your boots Master Jeremy, I've never seen anything like them before. Rubber, are they?" asked Ned. "No cheap plastic, nothing special, just ordinary," replied Jack.

"Do they keep the water out?" asked Ned.

Tom fetched water from a pump outside and boiled it in an old dented rather dirty saucepan on the small fire which burned in the harness room.

"Here have a cup of char," Ned said handing Jack a tin mug, which somehow disappeared before it ever reached his hand, which pleased Jack as the brew inside looked extremely unpleasant and smelt strongly of saddle soap.

"So when do the horses go out," persisted Jack mainly because he knew that Matt would want to know, being interested in wars and horses and not much else.

"When your Uncle orders them to take him somewhere. But he doesn't go anywhere much being too upset by the war and losing his dog Ruffian, and his only son being killed at Flanders. He's not the man he was, Master Jeremy; his hair's turned white. But then you must have heard about Master Roderick, the apple of his father's eye, being killed. Didn't they tell you that at the school you go to? They must have done. You being so fond of him and all," said Ned.

And now suddenly Jack felt so utterly depressed and being only nine, he almost burst into tears.

"I'm all mixed up. I'm not Jeremy," he said wiping his eyes. "And I think you're ghosts."

"And at the word 'ghosts', everything but the cobwebs vanished, so that suddenly Jack found himself standing alone in a small room full of old beer cans and rubbish shrouded in cobwebs. Even the lantern was gone and there was no fire anymore in the old grate, just a long-dead mouse. And then he saw dozens of rats coming out of the corners and peering at him with bright eyes.

Trembling uncontrollably, Jack stumbled towards the stable door and forcing it open, ran outside shouting, "The stable's full of ghosts and rats and cobwebs, Mum. It's horrible, really horrible." And now his mother was there, holding out her arms to him. "And the poor horses are tied up all the time and they haven't any tails," continued Jack.

"It's all right Jack, it's just a bad dream and I'm here now," said his mother hugging him.

"It wasn't a dream; it was real and I was Master Jeremy. Ned and Tom kept calling me that. Who was he, Mum?" Jack asked.

A little later sitting in the kitchen which suddenly seemed incredibly light with the strip light shining bright from the ceiling, his mother said, "I thought you knew that my family lived here years and years ago Jack. Jeremy was my great grandfather. That's why we bought the house. Didn't we tell you?"

Jack shook his head. He wasn't

trembling any more. He was thinking, Matt will never believe me, not when I tell him.

"It was so real. Ned kept talking about the war and the horses going there and everyone getting killed. It was horrible Mum and so dirty and Tom the stable boy was smaller than me and already working. And then there were the rats. They came out when Ned and Tom had gone. I'm so glad I didn't live then," Jack said, drinking tea and remembering the drink he had been offered by Tom in the tin mug.

"What happened to Jeremy then?" Jack asked next.

"He died in the second world war," his mother said. "Try and forget all about it."

But Jack knew he wouldn't. What had happened was too real to forget. It would be with him for ever. And it wasn't just his imagination at work. He knew that now, because Jeremy had really existed. Before he went to bed his mother showed Jack a photograph of Jeremy, a slim handsome man smoking a cigarette, sitting astride a bay horse.

"I don't think I like the good old days any more," said Jack getting into bed. "Because they weren't good, they were really rather horrid. Do you think Matt will believe me when I tell him what happened."

"Probably not, but you will always remember it and that's what matters, Jack. Shall I leave the light on," asked his mother.

"Yes please, just for a bit," Jack said. "Just until I'm asleep," but even as he spoke, what had happened was growing less vivid in Jack's mind. When I'm older, he thought, I shall write it all down so that people will know what it was really like in the good old days and then Ned and Tom and Jeremy will never ever be forgotten. I might even make a film about it. Jack overslept the next day and when he looked out he saw that the stable had already been demolished and half of him was pleased and half of him was sorry. But most of all he was glad he had gone inside for one last look before everything, which had been there, vanished for ever.